COYOTE,

AND WOLF TALES

Contents

Native Americans have many stories about the coyote. This traditional tale comes from the Zuni people.

Coyote and Locust

A Native American Tale

Coyote went hunting.
He saw a locust sitting
in a tree, singing.

"I would like to sing like
you," said Coyote. "Teach me
your song."

Locust sang the song,
then Coyote sang it after him.

"What a good singer I am,"
said Coyote, and off he went
singing Locust's song loudly.

Coyote was so busy singing that he didn't see a hole. Coyote fell into it. When he got up, he had forgotten the song.

Coyote went back to Locust.

"Teach me your song again," he said.

Locust sang the song and Coyote sang, too.

"Don't forget it this time, Coyote," said Locust. "I won't teach it to you again."

Coyote went away, singing at the top of his lungs.

Coyote made a lot of noise as he sang. He sang so loudly that the birds flew out of the trees and frightened him.

"Silly birds," said Coyote. "You have made me forget the song. Locust will just have to sing it again."

Now Locust knew that Coyote would forget his song and keep coming back to be taught it again and again.

"I will teach Coyote
a lesson," he said.

So Locust shed his
skin on the tree trunk
and flew away.

Coyote came up
to the tree.

"Locust, you must
teach me your song
again," said Coyote.

Coyote waited,
but nothing happened.

Coyote got mad.

"Locust, if you don't teach me your song, I'll crunch you up," he shouted.

The locust shell was silent.

"I warned you," shouted Coyote, and he leaped at the locust shell.

He bit the locust shell hard, and his teeth broke on the hard trunk of the tree. Coyote howled and howled.

Ever since then, a coyote's middle teeth look broken, and a locust always sheds its skin.

Some of the best-known fox stories were told nearly 2,500 years ago by a man named Aesop.
Here is one of Aesop's fables.

The Fox and the Crow

An Aesop's Fable

One day, a fox saw a crow
fly off with some cheese
in its beak. The crow sat
on a wall to eat the cheese.

"I would like that cheese,"
said Fox. So Fox walked up
to the stone wall.

"Hello, Crow," said Fox.
"How beautiful you look today.
How black your feathers are.
How bright your eyes are.
You are the queen of all birds.
I am sure that you sing well,
too. Will you sing a little song
for me?"

The crow liked being
called the queen of all birds.
She lifted her head and began
to sing.

"Caw, caw, caw!"

But, the moment she opened her beak, the cheese fell from her mouth and was snapped up by Fox.

"That will do," said Fox. "Now, in exchange for the cheese, I will give you some advice. Never trust flatterers."

This Chinese fable teaches that it pays not to be boastful.

The Fox and the Crab

A Chinese Fable

One fine day, a fox went
to drink from the river. He saw
a small crab sitting on a rock.

"You are such a little animal,"
said Fox. "Can you run?"

"Yes," said Crab. "Sometimes
I run from the river up
to the grass and back again."

"Why, that is not really running. If I had as many legs as you, I would run as fast and as far as the wind. You are a stupid creature!" said Fox.

"I think it is your bushy tail that makes you such a fast runner," said Crab. "If you would let me tie down your tail, I think I could beat you in a race to the top of the hill."

Fox laughed at the idea of racing with Crab. But he agreed to the challenge.

"I will put a weight on your tail, then I'll call out 'Go!' and the race will begin," said Crab.

As Fox stood still, Crab went behind him and grabbed his tail with her claws.

"Go!" Crab shouted, and Fox ran as fast as he could.

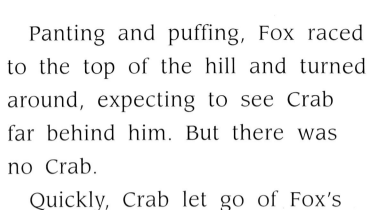

Panting and puffing, Fox raced to the top of the hill and turned around, expecting to see Crab far behind him. But there was no Crab.

Quickly, Crab let go of Fox's tail and dropped to the ground, calling out, "Good to see you, Fox. What took you so long?"

Fox turned back, and there, ahead of him on the path, was little Crab.

Ashamed, Fox hung his head and crept away.

Big, bad wolves feature
in many traditional tales.
The Cherokee Native Americans
tell this story about seven wolves
and a groundhog.

Dance of the Wolves

A Native American Tale

Once upon a time, seven wolves caught a little groundhog.

"Now we are going to eat you," growled the wolves.

"Tut, tut, tut!" scolded the groundhog. "Don't you know that you must always dance before you eat. That's what people do."

"Of course we know what to do," said the wolves. "We will dance like the people do."

So the wolves leaped, jumped, and pranced around the little groundhog.

"Dear, dear," said the groundhog. "What bad dancers you are. I can see I will have to teach you how to dance."

"Now, when I sing, you must dance away from me. When I say the word 'Yu', you must run towards me. Then, when I start to sing again, you must dance away. Do you understand?"

The wolves all nodded.

"Start singing," they snarled.

So the groundhog sang and the wolves danced away.

"Yu," shouted the groundhog, and the seven wolves raced back towards him. But, before they could grab him, the groundhog started to sing again.

Over and over, he sang the song, and the wolves kept dancing and running and dancing and running.

At last, the groundhog could see the wolves were getting tired. This time, the groundhog sang for longer, and the wolves danced further and further away. The groundhog ran as fast as he could to his burrow.

"Yu," he shouted, and dived into the hole.

The wolves stopped dancing.
They raced to the groundhog.
One wolf caught the groundhog's
bushy tail just as he disappeared.
The wolf bit the groundhog's tail
right off.

And a groundhog's tail
has been short ever since!

Tales and Fables

People have always enjoyed telling and listening to stories and tales. Traditional tales often give reasons for why things are the way they are. Stories that contain a lesson, or a moral, are called fables.

Both tales and fables often show foxes and wolves as cunning, boastful, and cruel. In Native American tales, coyotes are sometimes clever, sometimes stupid, and sometimes tricksters that end up in trouble.